Cyril's Cat and the Big Surprise

Shoo Rayner

PUFFIN BOOKS

Published by the Penguin Group
Penguin Books Ltd, 27 Wrights Lane, London W8 5TZ, England
Penguin Books USA Inc., 375 Hudson Street, New York, NY 10014, USA
Penguin Books Australia Ltd, Ringwood, Victoria, Australia
Penguin Books Canada Ltd, 10 Alcorn Avenue, Toronto, Ontario, Canada M4V 3B2
Penguin Books (NZ) Ltd, 182–190 Wairau Road, Auckland 10, New Zealand

Penguin Books Ltd, Registered Offices: Harmondsworth, Middlesex, England

Published in Puffin Books 1993
10 9 8 7 6 5 4 3

Filmset in Monotype Bembo Schoolbook

Reproduction by Anglia Graphics Ltd, Bedford

Made and printed in Great Britain by William Clowes Limited, Beccles and London

Contents

The Wonderful Smell   4

A Surprise for Cyril!   34

THE WONDERFUL SMELL

Cyril's cat Charlie was bored. He had been bored for two or three days. Cyril was worried about him. At supper time Charlie came into the kitchen and looked at his food.

Not that tinned stuff again, he thought. I'm so bored with the tinned stuff. Then he swished his tail and went outside to sit in the drizzling rain.

Cyril watched him through the kitchen window. "I wonder what the matter is," he said to himself. "Maybe he doesn't like his food. I'll see if I can get something nice for him tomorrow."

7

When Cyril got up the next
morning, Charlie still hadn't
touched his supper. Cyril gave him
a saucer of cream but Charlie
didn't even try it. Instead he
dragged himself through the cat-
flap and found a puddle to lie in.
Cyril didn't know what to do.

Charlie just lay in the puddle with
his eyes shut. He didn't even
twitch when a fly landed on his
whiskers. He heard Cyril close the
gate behind him, as he went off to
the shops, but he wasn't interested.
He was bored and fed up and that
was all there was to it!

Then Charlie's nose began to
twitch. He could smell something
just . . . well . . . wonderful, and it
seemed to come from over the
fence.

Charlie forgot that he was bored
and went off to investigate.

He squeezed through a hole in the fence and found Hercules, the cat who lived next door, keeping a watch on the bird table. "Can you smell anything?" asked Charlie.

Hercules lifted his nose high into the air and sniffed, first this way then that. "MMMMMM!" he sighed. "I can smell it all right. I think it's coming from over there."

The two cats walked to the bottom of the garden. They had one thing on their minds. Where was that wonderful smell coming from? They crossed six gardens and two roads. The scent was getting stronger.

They stopped in front of an old, rusty dustbin that someone had left on the pavement. This was where the wonderful smell was coming from.

The lid wasn't on properly so they climbed in. There was a lot of other rubbish, but they soon found what they were looking for.

Wrapped in a sheet of soggy
newspaper were the leftovers of a
poached salmon. It was yummy,
and they got to work on it as if
they hadn't eaten for days, which,
in Charlie's case, was true.

They were having such a good
time that they didn't notice the
dust-cart moving slowly down the
street. They didn't notice until
they were hurled into the back of
the dust-cart!

They landed upside down in a
heap of coffee grounds and potato
peelings.

They were very surprised and they
were trapped! The rubbish
cruncher was right behind them. A
wall of rubbish was in front of
them. They climbed up and up the
rubbish pile until they found a
hiding place right at the top. It
was dark and smelly. Charlie and
Hercules were not very happy.

23

They stayed there while the dust-
cart did its rounds, collecting the
rubbish. It seemed a very long
time before they were tossed out of
their hiding place into the bright
daylight and on to the mountain
of rubbish at the tip.

The driver of the dust-cart heard
an odd noise when he emptied out
the rubbish. He thought it sounded
like a pair of unhappy cats.

When he went to the back of the
truck he saw it *was* a pair of
unhappy cats! Charlie and
Hercules looked very sorry for
themselves. They smelled a bit too!

The driver knew Charlie quite well; he always said hello to him when they came round each week. He picked up the cats, put them in the cab and gave them a lift home.

"Well!" said Charlie. "That was
too much of an adventure for me.
I never want to see poached
salmon again." Hercules agreed.
They both went home to see if
they had been missed.

Cyril had been very worried about Charlie and was very happy when he came through the cat-flap. He was so pleased he didn't even notice that Charlie smelled like a rubbish tip!

"Oh, Charlie," Cyril sighed, "you had me so worried. I'm glad you are home. Look, I've got something special for your supper." He bent down and put a bowl in front of Charlie. "I got it specially," he continued, "because you haven't eaten properly for days. It's a little bit of poached salmon!"

A SURPRISE FOR CYRIL!

Cyril was worried about Charlie.
Charlie wasn't very well. He was
getting fatter and fatter. He was
getting slower and slower.

"Oh, Charlie," sighed Cyril, "I shall have to take you to the vet." He put the lock on the cat-flap so that Charlie couldn't get out of the house.

Click!

Whenever Charlie had to travel somewhere, Cyril would put him into a special basket that looked a bit like a cage. When Cyril brought it out from the cupboard under the stairs, Charlie would hear the basket creak and shoot off to find a good hiding place. That's why Cyril locked the cat-flap first!

But this time, when Charlie heard the noise of the basket, he barely twitched his ears. He didn't even complain when Cyril put him in the basket, which he'd lined with fresh newspaper.

They looked at each other
through the bars of the metal
door. "Oh, Charlie," sighed Cyril
again, "let's get going . . . see
what the vet has to say about
you."

"Well, Charlie," the vet said, in a business-like way, "let's see what the problem is." Then he felt Charlie's tummy. He prodded and poked, squidged and stroked and then he started to laugh! Cyril couldn't see what was funny.

"Well," said the vet, wiping a tear from the corner of his eye, "there's nothing to worry about. Charlie's quite well. In fact you will soon be surprised just how well he is!"

Then, still laughing, he gave Cyril some pills, which he said were vitamins that would help Charlie build his strength up.

When they got home Cyril tried
to give Charlie his vitamins. He
slipped one of the pills on to the
back of Charlie's tongue.

He held Charlie's mouth shut until
he thought he had swallowed it.

They looked at each other for a
while then Cyril let go.

With a gentle cough the pill flew
out of Charlie's mouth and shot
across the kitchen floor.

Cyril tried again and again but Charlie would not swallow the pill. Then Cyril crushed it up and mixed it with Charlie's favourite food. But Charlie wasn't interested.

He sat by the cat-flap and waited
for Cyril to unlock it, then he
headed straight for the shed and
squeezed into the space
underneath. And there he stayed!
He was still there when Cyril
came to see him the next morning.

"I suppose he's all right," Cyril
tut-tutted to himself. "The vet did
say I'd be surprised how well he'd
soon be. Perhaps he just needs to
be left alone to rest." So that's
what Cyril did. He left Charlie
alone. He went shopping, then
when he got back home, he made
his lunch. He had just sat down to
eat when he heard the sound of
the cat-flap.

55

It was Charlie. He was carrying a
tiny kitten in his mouth! He put
the kitten into his basket and gave
Cyril a big smile!

Cyril froze like a statue. His
mouth was open and his fork-full
of lunch stuck halfway between his
plate and his mouth. Charlie went
back through the cat-flap. He
came back a minute later, with
another kitten!

Charlie carried on, backwards and forwards, until there were four tiny kittens nuzzling up and drinking milk.

Cyril finally put his fork down and
roared with laughter!

"The vet was right," he said,
tickling Charlie between the ears.
"You really have surprised me. All
this time I thought you were a
boy and now, here you are, a
mummy with four dear little
kittens of your own! They'll all
need names, but first we'll have to
think of a new name for you!
Now . . ."

ready, steady, read!

Captain Daylight and the Big Hold-Up
  David Mostyn
Cyril's Cat: Charlie's Night Out *Shoo Rayner*
Farmer Jane *Gillian Osband* and *Bobbie Spargo*
Farmer Jane's Birthday Treat
  Gillian Osband and *Bobbie Spargo*
The Get-away Hen
  Martin Waddell and *Susie Jenkin-Pearce*
Hedgehogs Don't Eat Hamburgers
  Vivian French and *Chris Fisher*
The Little Blue Book of the *Marie Celeste*
  Angie Sage
The Little Green Book of the Last, Lost
  Dinosaurs *Angie Sage*
The Little Pink Book of the Woolly Mammoth
  Angie Sage
The Lucky Duck Song
  Martin Waddell and *Judy Brown*
Puffling in a Pickle
  Margaret Ryan and *Trevor Dunton*
Swim, Sam, Swim
  Leon Rosselson and *Anthony Lewis*